SHARE A STORY

"Have You Seen the Crocodile?"

Introduction

One of the best ways you can help
your children learn and learn to read
is to share books with them. Here's why:

• They get to know the **sounds**, **rhythms** and **words**
used in the way we write. This is different from how we
talk, so hearing stories helps children learn how to read.

• They think about the **feelings** of the characters
in the book. This helps them as they go about
their own lives with other people.

• They think about the **ideas** in the book. This helps
them to understand the world.

• Sharing books and listening to what your children
say about them shows your children that you care
about them, you care about what they think
and who they are.

Michael Rosen

Michael Rosen
Writer and Poet
Children's Laureate (2007-9)

First published 1986 by Walker Books Ltd
87 Vauxhall Walk, London SE11 5HJ

This edition published 2011

2 4 6 8 10 9 7 5 3 1

This book has been typeset in Optima

Printed in China

British Library Cataloguing in Publication Data:
a catalogue record for this book is available from the British Library

ISBN 978-1-4063-3516-3

www.walker.co.uk

"Have You Seen the Crocodile?"

Colin West

WALKER BOOKS
AND SUBSIDIARIES
LONDON · BOSTON · SYDNEY · AUCKLAND

"Have you seen the crocodile?" asked the parrot.

"No," said the dragonfly.

"Have you seen the crocodile?"
asked the parrot
and the dragonfly.

"No,"
said the
bumble bee.

"Have you seen the crocodile?"
asked the parrot
and the dragonfly
and the bumble bee.

"No," said the butterfly.

"Have you seen the crocodile?"
asked the parrot
and the dragonfly
and the bumble bee
and the butterfly.

"No," said the hummingbird.

"Have you seen the crocodile?"
asked the parrot
and the dragonfly
and the bumble bee
and the butterfly
and the hummingbird.

"No," said the frog.

"No one's seen the crocodile!"
said the parrot
and the dragonfly
and the bumble bee
and the butterfly
and the hummingbird
and the frog.

But then ...

"I'VE SEEN THE CROCODILE!" snapped the crocodile.

"Have YOU seen the parrot
and the dragonfly
and the bumble bee
and the butterfly
and the hummingbird
and the frog?"

asked the crocodile.

Sharing Stories

Sharing stories together is a pleasurable way to help children learn to read and enjoy books. Reading stories aloud and encouraging children to talk about the pictures and join in with parts of the story they know well are good ways to build their interest in books. They will want to share their favourite books again and again. This is an important part of becoming a successful reader.

Have You Seen the Crocodile? is a humorous story, told in a simple way to support beginning readers. The repetition helps children to read the words on their own and the surprise ending leaves them with something interesting to think about. Here are some ways you can share this book:

• The pictures help to tell the story but they also tell more than the words. Children will enjoy spotting the crocodile in the pictures long before it's mentioned in the words.

• Re-read the story together, pausing for children to read aloud the questions ("Have you seen the crocodile?") and the answers ("No.") as you read the rest. This is a good way for them to join in the reading and helps them to notice the patterns in the story.

• Once they know the book well, encourage children to read it for themselves. When they get stuck on a word you can help them to make a good guess by looking at the pictures, asking them what would make sense and looking at the beginning and ending of the word. Praise good guesses even if they don't match the word in the book. This helps build children's confidence to have a go.

• Talking together about the book increases children's enjoyment and understanding. What do they think happens in the end?

• You can act out the story together. This helps children to understand it and sequence it, and brings it alive for them.

SHARE A STORY
A First Reading Programme
From Pre-school to School

Beginnings – 2 years+

Look Out, Suzy Goose — Petr Horáček — Introduced by Michael Rosen

Walking Through the Jungle — Julie Lacome — Introduced by Michael Rosen

Hello, Goodbye — David Lloyd, Louise Voce — Introduced by Michael Rosen

Ten in the Bed — Penny Dale — Introduced by Michael Rosen

This Is the Bear — Sarah Hayes, Helen Craig — Introduced by Michael Rosen

The Big Wide-Mouthed Frog — Ana Martín Larrañaga — Introduced by Michael Rosen

Early Steps – 3 years+

A New House for Mouse — Petr Horáček — Introduced by Michael Rosen

The Train Ride — June Crebbin, Stephen Lambert — Introduced by Michael Rosen

The Other Day I Met a Bear — Russell Ayto — Introduced by Michael Rosen

Old MacDonald Had a Farm — Jane Chapman — Introduced by Michael Rosen

The Tiger and the Jackal — Vivian French, Alison Bartlett — Introduced by Michael Rosen

Zed's Bread — Mick Manning, Brita Granström — Introduced by Michael Rosen

Next Steps – 4 years+

The Hairy Toe — Daniel Postgate — Introduced by Michael Rosen

The True Story of Humpty Dumpty — Sarah Hayes, Charlotte Voake — Introduced by Michael Rosen

Beans on Toast — Paul Dowling — Introduced by Michael Rosen

Over in the Meadow — A Counting Rhyme — Louise Voce — Introduced by Michael Rosen

Dog Blue — Polly Dunbar — Introduced by Michael Rosen

Night-night, Knight And Other Poems — Michael Rosen, Sue Heap — Introduced by Michael Rosen

Taking Off – 5 years+

"Have You Seen the Crocodile?" — Colin West — Introduced by Michael Rosen

Handa's Surprise — Eileen Browne — Introduced by Michael Rosen

The Ravenous Beast — Niamh Sharkey — Introduced by Michael Rosen

One, Two, Flea! — Allan Ahlberg, Colin McNaughton — Introduced by Michael Rosen

Dinosaurs' Day Out — Nick Sharratt — Introduced by Michael Rosen

The Old Woman and the Red Pumpkin — Betsy Bang, Rachel Merriman — Introduced by Michael Rosen

Sharing the best books makes the best readers

WALKER BOOKS

www.walker.co.uk